I0629689

THE WORLD AND GOD

THE WORLD AND GOD

DEJAN STOJANOVIĆ

Translated by
Željko Mitić

New Avenue Books

THE WORLD AND GOD
English translation Copyright © 2024 New Avenue Books

This book was originally published in Serbia, Belgrade, in 2017 by UKS (The Association of Writers of Serbia) under the title *Svet i Bog* as the second book of the pentalogy *The World in Nowhereness* (Serbian: *Svet u nigdini* and a subtitle Pentalogija: *Ozar, Svet i Bog, Svet u nigdini, Svet i ljudi, Dom svetlosti*).

All rights reserved. Printed in the United States of America.
No part of this book may be used or reproduced in any form without written permission from the publisher, except in the case of brief quotations embodied in critical articles and reviews.

New Avenue Books
&
Albatros Plus

First Edition in English

Library of Congress Control Number: 2024950408

ISBN-13: 979-8-9916352-6-4

THEY SAID ABOUT *THE WORLD IN NOWHERENESS*

"When I got my hands on Dejan Stojanović's book *The World in Nowhereness*, I was amazed and read the book with great pleasure. I did not even believe there was someone today who could write such a long poem, an epic, as if I opened to read the *Iliad* in our time. I recommend this book to all believers in poetry because faith in poetry is the same as faith in eternity and eternal life."

— *Matija Bećković*

"*The World in Nowhereness* is Dejan Stojanović's utopian absolute book, a Mallarméan absolute. An absolute story, or an absolute book, according to Borges, is a desert-like book: sandy, grainily unforeseeable, and corpuscularly innumerable. It is simultaneously a vision and a chimera. Isn't that precisely why we long for an absolute book? *The World in Nowhereness* by Dejan Stojanović is, in his way, an embodiment of that dream."

— *Srba Ignjatović*

"I have always wondered, even about my poetic work, what a total poem is… Can the pentalogy by Dejan Stojanović be called a total poem that every poet of note has dreamed about since Homer? I felt such impulses while reading *The World in Nowhereness*. This is an absolute poem, of an absolute system of thought that reaches across the totality of our civilizational legacies."

— *Duško Novaković*

"Exactly 17 years ago, in the last year of the 20th century, I came across the work of Dejan Stojanović, and then I wrote a text from which I will extract a few sentences. "Dejan Stojanović, in the last two years, made a real feat; he published six books, except for one, all books of poetry." This first five-book collection was published in the last year of the 20th century, and here we are now with the five-book collection in the XXI century, nearing the end of the second decade. And then I also wrote the following: "Stojanović is a poet who searches for the perfect poetic form because at the same time he searches for the absolute meaning of human existence." Whether it was a hunch or not, there is the Pentalogy, and there is that word, that concept – an absolute, an absolute book, an absolute poem that could be sensed even in that first pentalogy, in those poems that he published at that time."

— *Aleksandar Petrov* (January 17, 2018)

"(*The World in Nowhereness* offers) the joy of cognition due to discoveries worthy of the Nobel Prize…"

— *Milan Lukić*

"*The World in Nowhereness* is primarily the result of great literary ambition and faith in literature. It was not only Kiš who said that literature is created by form and that Sartre's quote should be placed at the entrance to the Association of Serbian Writers that "someone does not become a writer to say certain things, but to say them in a certain way." Dejan Stojanović is one of those who think well about that way and think very sovereignly and broadly. Even in how he approaches the form, we can see the breadth of his education, including the humanities and the natural sciences. However, perhaps more than anything else, he enters into some area of spirituality and, I would even dare say, esoteric. If you read Dejan Stojanović, your life will not be the same – it will be better."

— *Muharem Bazdulj*

"It has been quite a while since we had, if at all, a poetic pentalogy in Serbian poetry."

— *Dušan Stojković*

Dejan Stojanović's poetic-philosophical book *The World in Nowhereness*, both in form and content, is an original and exceptional literary work and can be considered a rare literary event in Serbian poetry and on the world stage.

— *Nevena Vitošević*

"It is every poet's dream to write a relevant, unique, comprehensive book in which he will properly present all his thoughts and feelings that have appeared in his long conversations with the world. By the *world,* I mean everything manifested and abstract in (a) language, what is named, and what can be named. Dejan Stojanović's extensive pentalogy *The World in Nowhereness* is an attempt at writing such a book. This pentalogy about the world and light is an ambitious endeavor."

— *Bratislav R. Milanović*

"*The World in Nowhereness*, the pentalogy by Dejan Stojanović, is an unusual endeavor in Serbian literature."

— *Nikola Marinković*

"*The World in Nowhereness*, a poetic endeavor by Dejan Stojanović, is an exceptional occurrence in Serbian."

— *Dragan Kolarević*

"There are very few such books in Serbian literature."

— *Ivan Cvetanović*

"(The publishing of *The World in Nowhereness* is) a significant date in contemporary Serbian poetry."

— *Miljurko Vukadinović*

"Steadfast and consistent, with his mapping out of circular trajectories in the realms of poetry and philosophy, and always being something more than the sum of all parts, Dejan Stojanović has proved to be a thinker of continuously inventive thought. He belongs to that creative ilk whose body of work affirms the permanence of the long-established unity of the Mystic and the Magus. On the one hand, he is one of those with extensive knowledge and who, according to Bela Hamvash, are Mystics. Yet, he is also one of the Magi, who also possesses knowledge, but one meant to encourage and reflect the urge to peer into the other, lesser-known or completely unexplored side, which light cannot reach at first glance."

— *David Kecman Dako*

Dejan Stojanović, a sincere devotee of both poetry and philosophy, achieved a real poetic feat in 2017 by publishing an extensive five-volume book titled *The World in Nowhereness*.

— *Aleksandar B. Laković*

"The author is deeply immersed in his attempt to decode the essence of the universe, the meaning of the origin, and the persistence of being therein. He seeks balance and the possibility of introducing harmony into seemingly incompatible, disharmonious phenomena and concepts."

— *Gordana Vlahović*

"Dejan Stojanović offers us *The World in Nowhereness*, his latest book, as a spiritual anthology. This is an ambitious poetic and essayistic project in a predominantly philosophical, dense, and layered pentalogy about humanity as the source and the final destination of all visible and invisible worlds. The manuscript is presented in innovative, avant-garde form. Dejan Stojanović wisely and expertly intertwines poetry and prose, the epic and the lyrical, and the theoretical-critical."

— *Zorica Arsić Mandarić*

"Stojanović's pronounced contemplativeness is what makes him stand out in the contemporary world of the poetic invention as one of the few being in no quandary about the equality of poetry and philosophy and the necessity of their proper understanding, as well as a deeper decoding of the meaning behind words. For that reason, I see his search in the book *The World in Nowhereness* as a quest for the meaning of elemental survival in a time that is alienated, brutally real, and preoccupied with everything and nothing."

— *Vidak Maslovarić*

"Stojanović's poetic, prosaic, and dramatic approach represents, in a unique sense, an array of basic concepts and elements of human existence, its earthly and cosmic destiny. He tackles the subjects of freedom, the Absolute, God, the Devil, chaos, order, truth, the world, etc. The philosophical, the religious, and the poetic make up the basic core in the interpretation and understanding of the ontology of human survival."

— *Jovo Cvjetković*

Contents

THE WORLD AND GOD

PROEMIUM

ATOMS

The world awakens and sprouts from a concise idea, from the superelement in which all knowledge and memory sleep. Neither matter is what appears to the senses nor the idea of what the brain (the mind) thinks about it: the idea is matter, and matter is the idea. The idea must have weight and form to think and conceive of itself in the desolate sea. Matter would be deader than death without the idea that feeds its motionless motion because, as quantum mechanics teaches, there is no real movement.

Even the most minuscule speck carries within itself a spark of knowledge of the whole universe, which finds a sense of movement and path in its atoms. Without self-sufficient and self-conscious knowledge, every atom would evaporate before setting out on the path of self-realization to seek itself in the eternal truth from which it starts its journey. Every atom is a memory of the universal idea and a memory of itself. Every atom is a touch and a collision, a reflection of this memory and harmonization in the flow and shaping of the Being that seeks its sense in multitude, and in multitude sees salvation and a way out; a way out of itself, out of its slavery and its darkness. It will soar into nothingness, and it sees the conquest of darkness as the sole escape from being enslaved by its omnipotence, into the dark emptiness of freedom that offers hope because it offers a path into space and a way out.

Although merging and the unmistakable harmony are a sign of perfection, every collision and explosion are proof of the infallible harmony in which every particle finds its place. Seemingly accidental collisions and annulments lead to new elements and the true sources of life. From the fiercest annulments, the most potent force of life is born that conquers the darkness of nothingness and offers salvation and hope in movement and searching. There lies the whole explanation of the story of good and evil. There is neither good nor evil in itself: (there is) only a desolate sea that

5

fills everything and, with its sorrowful eye, lurks around the World that chooses life over death.

Life implies competition and growth; life implies taking a position and earning it in a struggle against other elements that dream and seek themselves on the same path. If life were pure justice and a pure reward (indeed, it is), there would be no point in seeking and finding oneself and the world while strolling toward sense.

Every pain and beauty reflect that sense and the price to be paid for the same sense, the price by which one obtains sense in the general flow of the organism that seeks and finds itself on the path of self-realization. Only pain knows the price of joy. Only darkness knows the value of light. Only evil knows the true happiness of good; only hatred knows the true power of love; only beauty encompasses the whole world, in all of its balance, and subsists on its light despite ascent or fall, despite the darkness, despite the pain, despite hatred and evil and, despite nothingness and death, it rises from the darkness to create and build a temple of beauty that, with the song of creation, defeats evil, darkness, and death itself.

PYRAMID OF THE WORLD

0
GOD
ZERO
UNITY
GOD AND ZERO
DIVISION OF GOD
BIRTH FROM CHAOS
DIVIDING & MERGING
HARMONY AND DECREES
BODY BRANCHING AND GROWING
A LOVE EMBRACE OF ZERO AND GOD
PATH THRU ZERO & OF ZERO THRU WORLD
THE ESTABLISHMENT OF GOD'S HIERARCHY
ZERO-GOD NUMBER-ZERO PASSAGE-INFINITY
PASSAGE AND EXIT INTO ONESELF – SPACE AND TIME
ETERNITY OF MOMENT & MOMENT OF WORLD'S ETERNITY
ZERO SPACE TIME INFINITY ETERNITY NUMBER INNUMERABILITY
ZERO INNUMERABILITY INFINITY GOD = DEVIL MULTITUDE FROM GOD

DARKNESS AND LIGHT

DARKNESS

The blackest point is the brightest star, but it conceals its light from
the darkness. Trapped within it and black, the light of the
condensed darkness sleeps,

Hiding from the darkness inside its darkness,
Fleeing into the darkness from the darkness,
Opposing the darkness with darkness
And sinking into its own farthest distance
Where even a non-being cannot find it
When it decides to sleep.
And so the light sleeps in its darkness
And so the darkness hides from darkness
And so the darkness preserves its light
And so the whole memory of darkness is contained in a point
And so the sky closes
And so time is captured
And so there is neither entrance nor exit
From the infinity of the compressed darkness;
And its huge infinity
Fills the world at the very brink of zero.
It is the sole truth,
For it is the biggest when it is alone
And cast (captured) into its very core.
And so darkness exists alone alongside the darkness
As they lurk around and wait for each other,
And so darkness thicker than darkness
Can always vanquish darkness.
Only its dark light can hide from the omnipotent darkness.

Before waking up, light is blacker than darkness. When the real
darkness decides to open its eyes, it opens itself before the

darkness and allows it to spread from zero into it, and darkness opens before it to receive this breadth, created from within, because infinite breadth, born from within, requires a huge space from outside. Thus, light is born –

> It opposes the darkness
> With darkness stronger than darkness
> And with light stronger than light

The Father is hiding – inaccessible even to the darkness itself, and the rebelling son steals the captured light and no longer hides from the darkness but engages in a battle with it – a battle that the darkness awaited, a battle it was dreaming about, for alone, without light, it was nothing:

And that is why this is not a rebellious angel
And that is why this is not the Fall
And that is why there is nothing like the Father
Who prepares his son for rebellion
Who prepares his son to remove Him
From the Black Throne
To become alive and open his eyes through the son by killing the
Father (himself)
To achieve sense from the dormant omnipotence;
From omnipotence, that is nothing
Precisely because it is omnipotent.
One has to pay the price for everything.
He has to dethrone himself
To accept justice and injustice
To accept fire and wandering
To accept beauty and horror
To realize the only possible world
From the waking light
From the fire stronger than any hell

Because there is no other hell
Because there is no other paradise

"Fire is only possible in this world – more intense than any book illustration, with innumerable fiery cauldrons and various glowing monsters, from quark to quasar. What hell, from books, can be stronger and bigger than this hell? What other hell in another world can produce more terrible and stronger fire than this one? What other world, in another world or life, can produce billions of living species that live on a single, tiny planet, nourished by a single, tiny sun, in an infinite sea with innumerable similar islands?

Fear of hell is nonsense. The only threatening fire is this world, while in another world, there is nothing but the darkness of an icy paradise and dead perfection. Wherever there is life, there is motion; wherever there is motion, there is a struggle. In every struggle, mistakes are made; wherever there is life, there is inequality; wherever there is inequality – there is no complete justice; where there is no complete justice, someone lags; wherever someone lags, pain is born; wherever there is pain, there is sorrow.

Injustice breeds jealousy
Jealousy breeds deception
Deceptions breeds hatred
Hatred breeds evil
Evil breeds hell

But all this belongs to pure mathematics – for the totality of the world to last, shine, and rejoice, all this must be paid – so that the darkness would begin to shine. And in paradise, there is nothing except for the captured light. That is why my son is the true ruler of darkness: light steals and overtakes (catches up with) the darkness and searches for it until the very end. That is why I accept the price, and that is why you, willy-nilly, have to accept the price because that is your only hell and heaven. That is your only world. And despite sometimes being terrifying and heavy, the world is magnificent in its beauty:

Nothing ever dies
You are eternal
Always and forever
Just like me
Agreeing with my downfall
To give you light (life)
And to watch you from the light –

The world is the price of light."

NOTHING AND SOMETHING

NOTHING

How large nothing is;
That nothing in size
And how small, non-existent,
And how that small, non-existent,
Has such power
To endow with size
Both the large and the small.
Without nothing
Both the small and the large would be nothing.
The bigger is bigger just because
It has more nothing within,
And the small is small with a little nothing within.
It is not known what is really big and small
Because nothing is just nothing
And it is ever the same,
And if we take nothing away from something
Then that something also disappears,
No matter how small or large it is.
How alive that nothing is
Awaiting an opportune moment from the darkness
And how large the light is
That looks for it in the darkness.
Without nothing, light has nothing to move into
And nothing to hope for
Nor can it land on a face
And lighten it with joy
And the light desires to bring joy;
Its happiness shines from radiant faces.
Despite being nothing, nothing is the home of light;
Despite being nothing, nothing is the house of darkness;
Despite being nothing, nothing is its own sense and hope;

Nothing is more patient than nothing,
Nothing more modest and humble,
Nothing more sublime in purity
Because nothing can be polluted,
Nothing is more sinless
Because nothing can sin,
Nothing is smaller or larger,
Nothing holier
Than the very nothing in the realm of emptiness.

SOMETHING

Even something is nothing without nothing.
Something sleeps until nothing begins to see from within it.
And even if there were not nothing, something would be
    something,
But without nothing, something would disappear
In its own oblivion;
There would be no one to awake and revive it;
Without nothing, this difference would be insignificant
Because something would be something
That cannot be born and come to life.
Still, the difference is not great;
Both before and after, something is nothing.
With nothing, something is something;
With something, nothing is something;
Without nothing, something is nothing;
Without something, nothing is nothing, after all.
Something moves into nothing,
Nothing begins to see out of something,
Light is born from the darkness of nothing.
Something without nothing is blacker than darkness.
Nothing is neither black nor white;
It is just something infinitely black;
Not even light can pass through it;
Without nothing, it can neither
Give nor receive light;
It is the very condensed core of darkness.
And when nothing begins to see from it
And starts to sing
And dissolves
And takes in
That small-big nothing

Gives birth to the world –
And light is born
And something gains eyes
And it can look into the space
And it can receive and emit light
And it is no longer the condensed darkness
But the condensed pure light.
The core of light is condensed darkness
And the Father dethrones himself,
From the omnipotent throne of darkness
Where everything is perfect
In perfect darkness
And the son puts himself on the throne of Light
Where perfection is in motion,
Wandering and falling,
Where perfection is in imperfection
Because that is the only hope.
Imperfection lends a hand to life.

NOTHING AND SOMETHING

Something sleeps in nothing;
Nothing waits in something;
Something is born out of nothing;
Nothing comes to life in something;
Those are the two main lovers;
The world is born from their embrace;
It is that omnipotent peace
And omnipotent dormant goodness
And omnipotent dormant beauty
And an omnipotent dream
The gentle harmony of being and non-being.
Both that peace and that gentle harmony
Are born only from howls, bangs, and chaos
To seek sense and salvation on the path through nothing,
To find beauty on the path through nothing,
To rejoice in its sunrises and sunsets,
Its storms and phases,
To find itself on its path,
Rescue itself from the dead sea of nothingness
And follow the love game of diverse beings,
To live its dream through their dream,
To see itself through their eyes,
To pray to itself with their words,
To absorb every letter and hear every note,
To remember everything,
Accept everything,
Both small and large,
Powerful and powerless,
To put everything in its place,
To offer consolation to everyone
With a vision of the big sky

And to whisper to them that the division is temporary,
That we are all the same and one in the great sea
And to swim in the omnipresent harmony of the born beauty.

HEAVEN AND HELL

HEAVEN AND HELL

"You are my hell and heaven," says God to his world,
"You are my *raison d'etre,* my destiny and glory,
You are my son and my beauty, you are my life
And hope. Every dimension sings inside you;
I melt myself into the world and seek myself from inside the
    world;
I am the thread that feeds the whole concise idea;
There is no me outside the world, nor the world outside me;
There is no hell outside heaven, nor heaven outside hell;
Hell is the most heavenly thing in the world.
Only from chaos and hell is it possible to create
Life and height, and to build a path to nothing.
Fire feeds life; heaven puts it to sleep.
I create hell in heaven and hell from heaven.
Hell is neither a threat nor a warning to the world;
Although the spring is heavenly, life is hellish;
Hell is a river; heaven is a spring that does not flow;
A spring may begin to murmur and a river to flow
Only when a spark of hell is kindled within God:
I offer you the life, o world, at a price that the world is to pay –

There is no life without light; there is no growth, beauty or
rejoicing, falling or rising, without a price. There is neither evil nor
good in itself – those are human interpretations. There is a world
that seeks, builds, and fixes itself; the world's beauty lies in
imperfection; the greatest perfection of the world is its
imperfection. The world's imperfection shows perfection in its
own symmetry; errors are not errors but interpretations;
explanations of the world and stories of good and evil, stories of
hell and heaven, are not evidence of hell or heaven. Your stories
impose laws and rules to introduce order and not to grasp the

essence; you are uninterested in the real truth of good and evil, of hell and heaven; you are interested in heaven and hell, good and evil, being prescribed, lest there would be no mistakes and deviations from the order or code of those who think it should be that way or that it is so much better that way.

And what is better? Is the truth a goal to be reached? Do those who hide behind God and speak on His behalf need God? My greatest enemies are those who speak on my behalf. I have never said anything to anyone in human words, but I've spoken the language of atoms, stars, flowers, and every living creature all my eternity. I speak and sing from everything; everything speaks and sings from me. No one knows my whole truth except for the entire world that narrates me and senses the truth. I, too, forget my truth so that I can more easily endure loneliness and the path – that I can rejoice in my light and find comfort in my hell, in my heaven, in my world that shines above hell and heaven with a light born out of my heart.

My heart is the source,
My heart is the ground from which the root of the universe grows,
A flower of light sprouts from my heart;
My heart feeds the light and knows the price
Of every pain that feeds the light
And the joy of every atom, grass, dragon, and person.
Truth never kills beauty –
Beauty grows from the heart of the truth;
An abandonment of truth is a betrayal of beauty;
With lies, one can neither defeat evil nor conquer beauty.
Good doesn't sleep in nice bedtime stories;
Lullabies offer neither day nor life,
Only good sleep.

But no lullaby claims to tell the truth, nor that I sing it; the only goal of a lullaby is sleep. Every story that offers sleep in the daytime that offers oblivion instead of confrontation, that deceives itself as well as others, that sings the sad tale of its helplessness is neither mine nor from me, nor do I agree with it.

The world has enough strength to endure itself,
Enough light to grow from itself,
Enough reason to understand the sense
And to find itself in senselessness, to regenerate itself
And rise above the law fueled by weakness.

The world does not need to put itself to sleep;
The world was born to live, to dream while being awake, and to
    see and understand inside the dream.
Every Divine secret is justified; there are no secrets except
    For the Divine ones,
There are no other worlds except for the Divine ones.
God neither threatens nor punishes anyone;
The world rewards and punishes itself;
God prescribes neither human punishment nor reward.
There is no need to invoke God to impose Order;
Imposing order by referring to God is a reflection of weakness
    rather than strength;
Strength radiates from itself;
Strength does not need God as an excuse;
True strength believes in God without the mediation of God;
God nourishes true strength that speaks from God, and God speaks
    from it, without words;
True strength proves God through action;
The word of true strength is a deed, not a word;
God is not God because He is so-called;
Every word is human.
Faith in God is not faith because it is proclaimed;
Faith in God is growth, harmony, feeling God at every step, and
    in every step.

God is not loved and worshiped only in a church;
The only God's Church is the World;
God is the World, and this Church is Holy;
God is both the Church and the World;
God looks from everything and in everything;
The whole World is the Altar of God;
The only dome of God is heaven;
Every step is recorded.

There is no hidden sin or the need for redemption before the preacher – there is no unanswered confession. But there is neither punishment nor guilt; sin and guilt are human concepts. I do not participate in everything as expected; the world punishes and corrects itself; there is no unpunished sin or guilt, but my math and harmony are not readily visible; faith is required because it gives birth to peace. Holy books contributed most to the extinction of faith. Before sacred books, as a form of prescribing God, everyone had faith; every person is by nature a believer and a seeker of God, whom he seeks within himself. The greatest world religions drive God out of people.

The ruling religions steal God from people; they don't encourage belief but fear. No office can declare and prescribe ownership over Almighty God; neither the Bible nor the Koran have an exclusive right to God; the whole Western world needs to return to God; it is more pagan to steal God from people and put Him in a book than the old paganism was. The only God's Bible is His big World that expands through infinite space. The world alone is not big enough to describe God; there are not enough atoms in the universe to write the Book of God. But the world exists, which is a huge, unread book containing every answer. The world offers both an answer and hope; the world is a story that tells God. Life is God's conversation with the world and human beings.

One can write and talk about God and be in books, but God cannot be prescribed; God is nobody's property. Such religions created the idea of hell in both this world and the next. God warms and nourishes the world with His light; He rejoices in His every form and being and wishes no evil; a threat of hell is the greatest imaginable evil. What kind of God would slaughter His children or burn and torment them in hell? What kind of God charges the admission price for heaven or hell? What kind of God would He be if He would burn Himself in hell, for every speck and every shape and every being in hell is God? There is nothing outside of God: every child is in God, of God, with God, and God is in everything.

Life is hell. Everything in life pays the price of life. Everyone redeems and rewards themselves; life is the greatest reward, while hardship, punishment, and injustice are part of the universal flow and proof of value. Without these elements, life would lose its value and beauty. The perfect world is dead. The world accepts the price of life and leaves its paradise; God accepts the price of light and the price of evil and sin. The world willingly leaves the blissful garden of paradise to bathe in the hell of Life. Life is the price of light – life is lived and sacrificed. Without sacrifice, there is no life. The world willingly sacrifices paradise for life.

People shall leave the cage where people, not God, placed them. The one human religion is God alone; a religion that steals God from people is not a religion. If people return to themselves, they will return to God. The path to God leads through oneself. God's greatest and most beautiful word is the voice of conscience speaking from within."

HEAVEN

Dream heaven is just dream heaven.
The only possible heaven is nothing without the world within.
Only nothing, devoid of the world, can be sinless.
Only nothing can be pure and sacred.
God is entirely pure only as long as nothing is outside of Him.
But then God vanishes in His purity,
He vanishes in the purity of nothingness;
Then God identifies Himself with nothing;
Nothing has no chance to sin;
God is a dormant justice;
He neither has a chance to sin without anything;
That is the only sinless heaven;
That is the only righteous justice
But a God who does not create is not a God;
A God who does not transform Himself, who does not bear
    Himself from Himself, is not a God;
The righteous justice of a dormant God is neither righteous nor of
    God;
It is the justice of the nothingness that sleeps within Him
And the nothingness in which He sleeps;
Only a God who accepts the price is the true God,
Only God who can err is the true God,
Only a God who rises from nothingness knows the price of fire, the
    price of rise and fall;
Only a dreaming God can give birth to heaven.
A dreaming God does not want a dormant and pure heaven;
God knows that it's easy to be sinless
Righteous and clean when everything is nothing
And when nothing is everything;
God does not want a tedious paradise of realization
In which there is only nothing to keep Him company;

God overcomes Himself and the nothingness in Himself,
He rises against the peaceful and righteous nothingness;
He has to pollute nothing to give it life
And to pollute Himself from the polluted nothing
So He would light up;
The world is the fire of heaven, and heaven is the fire of the world;
There is no heaven devoid of fire;
Fire does not look heavenly, but it is heavenly;
Heaven without fire is sad, tedious, and alone;
To burn in the fire, and to suffer, and to fall,
And to be tortured – all is better than not to be;
That is the justice of fire and the justice of the world
Which burns and lives; a world without fire is dead;
A world in which there is no sinning is sinful;
God is the greatest sinner
For He accepts His fall,
He sacrifices His heaven and absolute justice
In the name of the life that He chooses;
God accepts injustice towards Himself
And He turns Himself into a sinner
So that the fire would glow.
Absolute justice extinguishes justice,
Absolute innocence extinguishes life;
Every birth is somewhat sinful;
It's easy to be a dormant God,
It's easy to be a sinless God,
It is easy to be a righteous God,
It isn't easy to accept the awakening,
It's difficult to steal the fire,
It's difficult to sacrifice yourself for the fire,
It isn't easy to accept the right to err,
It is difficult to accept injustice yet to be just
And above the justice.
God is God

Because He lives above the justice,
Above the sinlessness,
Above the purity, above the fire
But He chooses His fall instead of His sinlessness,
Instead of His purity,
Instead of His justice,
He chooses life instead of death
And that's why it descends into life,
He chooses the multitude instead of His sad height,
He chooses a multitude that dreams and aspires to heights;
God's fall is His greatest height,
Through His Fall, God exceeds His height,
His righteousness,
His purity,
His sinlessness;
Through His fall, God overcomes emptiness.
The world is the love-embrace of God and emptiness;
The conception of emptiness is not sinless.
The world is born from the violation of emptiness
But emptiness has awaited its conqueror;
The emptiness longed to be violated;
God would remain the greatest sinner
Had he not satisfied the sad emptiness –
Sad, He would disappear in sinful sinlessness.
Emptiness saves God from Himself.
Without fertilizing emptiness, God becomes the same as it is.
He chooses life instead of nothingness.

HELL

What is brighter and more hellish than life,
What is more joyful and sublime;
Is there fire anywhere except in life,
Is there anything more beautiful than light?
It is not hell but life.
They frighten you in vain with eternal torment;
Eternal torments do not exist except in stories;
God is not that cruel and merciless;
Every torment is His,
Every pain is His,
Every sin hurts Him;
God does not punish;
The world lives and repairs itself,
It puts itself in order and redeems itself;
Both the smallest and the largest mistake,
The smallest and the greatest evil
Are wounds on the body of God.
Fire is the tongue of God that warms the emptiness of heaven;
Without hellfire, heaven would be sad and alone;
Fire gives birth to both beauty and sin,
Fire gives birth to glory and power,
Fire also gives birth to a fall,
Fire elevates and fire destroys,
Fire gives birth to both life and death;
Only the ignorant are afraid of fire,
Only the ignorant are leery of hell;
The most sublime act is the birth of fire;
The only way to overcome emptiness is Fire;
With hellfire, God overcomes nothingness,
And only nothingness is completely heavenly;
Only in nothingness does nothing happen;

In nothingness, there is neither light nor heat;
In heaven, even God dies of cold;
The only salvation of God is to escape from the paradise of
    nothingness
By stirring up the fiery thought.
God is a rebel who steals light,
Who does not agree to an icy paradise,
Who kindles fires all around,
Who offers salvation through torment and pain
But also through infinite beauty.
He agrees on the price and chooses life.

GOD AND THE DEVIL

THE PATH OF GOD

Like everything else, even God, who is everything, must pay the price when he sets out on a journey.

Only a cold God is absolutely righteous. A loving God accepts the price.

The face of fire and change is the face of God, who dethrones Himself.

A dead God is a unity; a living God is a duality.

No one can steal God's fire.
No one can rebel against God.
God rebels against Himself.

Regardless of how much they love God, they still diminish His strength; He has no son or children; there are no insurgencies in His kingdom; He is everything. He is the unity in innumerability and the innumerability in unity. The only insurgent (whom people named the Devil mistakenly) is He.

GOD IS PERFECT

God is perfect, and only nothing is perfect.

Going to heaven is the path to the ice of perfection.

Awakened nothing is life – a God divided by the storm.

They accuse God of being unjust and no true perfection, and He runs away from it – from the frozen, motionless sleep.

God is not utterly righteous because He rebels against Himself. Being the only rebel, He is alone.

God thunders and kindles fires to endure and vanquish the eternal nothing in Himself.

If the fire is the measure of hell, then the World is hell. There is no hell with more fire and energy apart from this world or bigger dragons in the netherworld apart from the black holes in this one.

GOD

God is the word that represents the almighty essence. The almighty essence cannot be outside itself; creation cannot be outside the creator; there is nothing outside him; and if there is nothing outside him, every creation stems from him; every creation is his transformation.

The world is the almighty essence and part of the almighty essence; the world is only the path of God to oneself through oneself; the world is a reflection, movement, reversal, awakening, and growth. If God is God, no matter how imagined, He must be everything. The very word signifies omnipotence. Any separation of the creator from the creation is blasphemy, misunderstanding, and contradiction in itself; every interpretation and mediation is blasphemous as well.

God converses with the world from every form and in every form: a conversation with Himself from the multitude. God never teaches anyone directly or interprets and retells Himself, nor does He offer Himself to select individuals more than to any other; He is equally accessible and close to everyone, although some do anticipate him more clearly. But He doesn't whisper stories in anyone's ear nor seek representatives on Earth, nor would He rejoice in so many divisions and atrocities committed in His name and so many lies.

God does not need prophets or holy books because no one has the exclusive right to Him. Many earthly religions are not interpretations of God but an exclusive "right" to Him and a negation of His primary essence and greatness; they are diminishment and belittlement of God. Those who accept their interpretations must also accept their God. Thus, it is not a matter of faith in God but of faith in interpretations and stories that "reached the ears of the chosen and the consecrated directly." God does not need to be attested; one must look left and right. Books must be accepted without any verification because "that's what God said. " And who claims to speak as God has spoken? Who has heard him? And what proof do we have of that?

There is no more sacrilegious interpretation of God than in the holy books. What could be more offensive to Almighty God than claiming an exclusive right to Him? In that way, He becomes a commodity and someone's property, and no one can claim ownership over God.

We are only a part of his garden, but that does not diminish the possibility of spreading stories that this or that was just like that; this happened just like this, this must be just like this, and there can be no other way, for God said so.

THE DEVIL

Who needs the Devil? God or people? God has no duality: God is One, and God is Innumerable; One in Innumerability; Innumerability in One. Through the Devil, holy books insult God, ascribing to the Devil a power he does not have. The only power of the Devil is the word that people have invented. Who can rebel against God and disrupt his math? How can anyone dare to ascribe so much power to anything and diminish the Almighty with stories about the Devil and his power, which puts him almost on a par with God?

Here, there is yet another mistake in the interpretation and appropriation of God. God becomes what people say He is and not what He is. Any interpretation of God outside this canon is interpreted as an attack on God. The greatest negation of God are the holy books: according to them, there is no God outside them. What could be a greater negation of God than fitting the whole God into several books? And God cannot fit into sentences and descriptions. Turning God into the property of any party, making promises of heaven on His behalf, making threats of hell on His behalf, provoking wars in the name of the kingdom of heaven – that seems more like the work of the devil than the work of God.

The only real rebel is God. Nobody except emptiness can oppose God. Only emptiness, or nothingness, plays a game with God, which God rules. He is the only one to steal the fire and give birth to fire from emptiness; He is the only rebel who rebels against darkness and emptiness. Only darkness and emptiness are pure. By creation, God disturbs the original peace:

He is that original explosion
The cosmic fireworks
He is the fog, height, and beauty
But also horror and terror
He turns Himself into innumerable characters

He seduces and reveals
He feeds every herb and every beast
Every snake and lamb

The Devil did not create the snake, the tree of knowledge and idea of good and evil, or the woman, and neither is God angry with His children on whom He bestowed freedom to seek themselves on their path, nor does He think of justice in human terms. God's justice does not come from human logic, and human logic is more remote from God's logic than the logic of ants is from human logic. It is not easy to vanquish nothing; it is not easy to give birth to sense and motion.

Almighty justice can only be death, for only death is perfect, and nothing in life can be perfect. Perfection lies in imperfection, in lack of absolute justice: absolute justice leads to immobility, and absolute justice implies absolute tranquility that is only possible in the original essence of the world. Every birth evokes a relationship between magnitudes, and in the relationship between magnitudes, a battle arises; in battles, there are defeats and victories; someone is bigger, and someone else is smaller. This is the simplest law of God that is overlooked. There is no justice as is understood in human terms; no one can offer to mediate in acquainting one with God, nor can they offer tickets to the kingdom of heaven. Any ticket box of this type is false, and all who approve them are deceivers, even though many are convinced they serve God, which does not redeem them.

There are billions of people opposed in beliefs among themself, ready to fight in the name of ideas from books describing God and Divine laws received from Him. And who were those who received these laws? Who authorized them to receive laws from God, to be his sole interpreters and preachers? In these things, authorization isn't necessary, they will say. And what is the difference between them and those who have never dared to do the same? What entitles them to be the ones who have the (exclusive) right to God? The right to His word and the interpretation of God? How small is God who can fit between the covers of (several) books. How insolent is the very intention to do so; how blasphemous it is to convey human stories and sell them as God's. The word of God is not human; people anticipate his language but do not understand it:

God is in everything
Everything is in God
God is the supreme seducer
God kindles fires and works miracles
Rebellion against darkness is God's rebellion
The only heaven is emptiness
Only emptiness is sinless
Only nothing is pure and peaceful
Nobody rules the darkness
The only ruler of the darkness is light
Only the darkness knows the price of light
Light is God's rebellion
God is the sole ruler of the darkness
Victory over darkness is *creatio diabolico*
The Devil can only be God
He is a builder
He is a conqueror
He raises alarms
He disturbs the weightless peace of emptiness
He is the rebellion against the nothingness of heaven.
Heaven is possible only in nothingness
There is no duality between heaven and hell
Just like there is no duality between God and the Devil
One duality arises from another
From the idea of life in this world and the next one
And from the idea of a better life in the next world
Duality offers fairy tales

Duality offers false relief
Avoiding the truth does not soothe the pain
It merely postpones it
Avoiding the truth does not cure the ill
It merely numbs it
Hope in a false world is not hope
A beauty concealed in the promises from stories is no beauty
Deception does not bring consolation
But it only puts hope to sleep
Hope is not hope
Hope is just a word
Hope is hope if one hopes for something certain
And not a hope that hopes in vain
Hope does not hope
It merely offers an unreal embrace
And it lulls the sight before the truth
That can awaken real hope
That can take a look at life
The only truth
The only fire
And fire is in life
Despite being hellish
Life is still fire, too
The next world is drowsiness
Only nothing has no price
Only something without a price can be heavenly
Only nothing is heaven
Life is the only hell and heaven
God is the only Devil
God rules life
And accepts the price
The price is in everything that we do not understand in God
In justice and injustice, in evil and good
And in His almighty beauty

That dreams of the world
And elevates to its throne
So that children would dream his dream
His life and only heaven
In this world
In this heaven
And they pray in their lives
For their life
Their only heaven
(Because) life is the only hope

THE DEVIL AND GOD

The Devil and God are synonyms. People invent words to present the meaning of different essences. However, people invent some words to deceive themselves and others, to overcome their impotence by false interpretations, and impotence cannot be overcome by inventing words and descriptions of the non-existent but by dealing with the actual.

All that exists, in one way or another, whether describable or indescribable, visible or invisible, deceptive or not, constitutes reality. The senses present reality within the limitations of their power; they show some of the innumerable faces of reality. The senses are a sincere possibility of experiencing reality outside of science and religion. The senses are the most important science, for they don't present anything non-existent. Even the impossible, when detected by the senses, reflects experienced or anticipated reality, even if everything the senses present is essentially different.

It is not deception but a reward
It is a gifted beauty
It is a possibility of a dream and a method to dream

It is the language that God uses while conversing with the world; those are the softened outlines of His being. Without this language, there is neither good nor evil, neither justice nor injustice, neither poverty nor wealth nor prestige nor vanity, neither hopes nor flights nor omnipotent beauty that laughs at senses from the surface. Every depth nourishes the beauty of the surface; every depth screams so that the surface can sing; every color caresses and quarrels with another so that the sight will have something to hope for. The whole world is an idea, and the entire world matters, although it differs from what the senses present. The whole world ripples and there is no division, no thoughts without bodies, and no bodies without thoughts.

The body of every ant is a thought and an idea; the body of every flower. Every flower and ant have more thoughts in themselves than the largest library. The ant looks differently, and the bat in the night of its ultra-sound; how proudly and distantly the eagle can look; and smells and touches and all the rest, in every type of various strengths. Everything leads to life and beauty. The real vision would be a loss of vision; the real vision dissolves reality, while the dissolved reality is in ripples, in invisible magnitudes. Since outside of the senses, there is no sight, touch, taste, hearing, smell, heat, or cold, it is only a program that determines the relationship to the world and matter.

Neither matter has to be what it is thought to be nor what the senses say about it. Can matter think? And if it does – what kind of matter is it? Or the very idea that thinks can incarnate itself, for, without incarnation, thought would not make much sense, and neither would the idea. Only an incarnated idea provides hope from the surfaces fed by depth. If the whole reality differs from how the senses present it, then there is no telling what real matter is or a real thought or idea. If the senses are programs that present different things differently to different beings, then it is possible to imagine a program of an incarnated idea. The energies of the idea manage to thicken and dilute its essence by rippling to introduce order into it because there is no right motion – there are only ripples.

There is no energy devoid of an idea, nor an idea devoid of energy – energy is a condensed idea. Matter is not condensed energy but a diluted idea. Illusion is what people refuse to accept, and that's the greatest truth; that is the devil's attire of God; it contains all His beauty and goodness, for God does not deceive us, but only Himself because it is a divine smile from the face of the World.

THE ABSOLUTE

CHAOS AND ORDER

A world before the world
God before God
God in nothing
Nothing in God
Undivided God
Uninhabited nothing
In His absolute order, God and nothing are the same
That is the only true order
Only within the undivided one does complete order reign
Only in the One and the uninhabited nothing does order rule
The only One equated with nothing is order
A realized existence is nothing
God is a realized existence
A realized existence is Non-existence
Only non-existence is the true order
The equation between God and nothingness is the easiest one
The realized world becomes its opposite
Realized World = Nothing
Nothing − Order
God = Nothing
Nothing maintains order both in order and disorder
God needs nothing for life and order
But God likes chaos the most
That is the devilish Divine trait
Every creation is devilish
Birth and life imply chaos
There is no life without disorder and chaos
Life is an eruption, fire, and power
Life flames, flies, builds, destroys
God's life force lies in his power
To destroy and create Himself

To give birth to Himself and life from the magma of His volcano
Chaos is born in the volcanic eruption of God
While God is only God, he sleeps
In absolute peace and dormant justice
His drowsiness is his order
This is the infallible God
The infallible God is a God without an exit
The infallible God is sorrowful
A God devoid of the chance of erring is
A God doomed to death
Only an erring God is the God of justice
An erring God chooses life
Instead of absolute justice and order
Only an erring God can be born and die
An erring God is a God of both chaos and order
The infallible God does not err because He cannot do so –
That is a dormant God

The first state of life is chaos and fire. Its strength is born and recognized in chaos; in chaos, it seeks forms and finds itself: everything is shattered into everything, and everything is mixed with everything; the circular motion begins in a firestorm. The movement of matter gives birth to a force of attraction – in circling, masses are attracted to the centers; circling gives birth to great and small worlds. Hierarchy maintains the balance of the world. It is established out of fire and chaos. The relationships between magnitudes are the first law of the universe; without this law, everything would escape into nothingness and die in sad equality.

THE ABSOLUTE

The true absolute is nothing – only death is absolute, but only what is born can die, and what is born is merely awakened, so there is no real death. That was the omnipotent everything, turned into nothing at the very apex:

Realized everything comes into nothing
Falling asleep in its opposite
Nothing lies in nothing
To find a dream in it
To erase and forget itself
So that it could find itself again
So that it could wake up again
So that it could hope again
So that it could search for itself on the road again
To find sense again on the path to Nothing
Nothing that lives can die
Nothing that starts can disappear
Nothing that hopes can stop
Seeking beauty awakened from the darkness.
The absolute becomes its opposite
The greatest power becomes impotence
It is the smallest when it is the largest
At the peak of its power, it turns into zero
It arrives in old nothing
To rest, not to disappear
To gather strength
To be able to hope again;
To multiply its truth
And arrange it into an uncountable number
And so zero becomes the biggest "number"
And so, nothing becomes the destination.

Blessed peace comes from nothing –
That's how it finds itself
That's how it transforms itself
That's how it loves and hopes
There lies all its strength
And its beauty

ZERO AND INNUMERABILITY

Zero is the beginning and end.
Without zero, there is no beginning or end
And without beginning and end
There can be no length or duration.
Does innumerability hide zero
Or does zero hide innumerability
Which is bigger: zero or innumerability?
The world has neither a beginning nor an end
But a world without a beginning and end is dead
A world that comes from nowhere
And it goes nowhere, is pointless
A world that has an unlimited path and growth
Disappears on its path
A world that cannot die is doubly dead
Dead in life and alive in death
A world that cannot be born dies of life
A world that cannot die,
Dies of death that cannot die
The past and the future are evidence of zero
Behind and before: the distances are evidence of zero
Innumerability cannot vanquish itself
Nor is it possible to imagine the final number
The only number imaginable
As the final one is zero
It is not possible to imagine the final number
On the path through the smallest number of seconds
It is always possible to divide further
But in the meantime, the past is taking place
The future has traveled its path through innumerability.
The smallest imaginable moment
That should be the present

But even that smallest moment
Can be divided into a new innumerability
When does the present take place?
Does it exist?
The present may never even happen.
Only the future passes through and goes on
Into the past through zero
Zero is the only moment
The only magnitude through which imagined
Or the measured time that does not exist
Deserves its existence
At least in thought
It seems that nothing lives in the present
Or that everything lives in the present
Or that zero deceives innumerability
Or that innumerability deceives zero
But either everything is only the past and the future
Or everything is the present
If there is the past and the future
The present is impossible
Because the present would capture
Both the past and the future
And thus, time and the world would stop
If there is only the present
Then zero merely dances with innumerability
To deceive both innumerability and itself
Zero, without innumerability, is alone and dead
Innumerability without zero is zero
Zero hides innumerability in itself
And innumerability hides zero
Zero annuls innumerability
And in that annulment, innumerability obtains life
Without zero, innumerability would be lost
And disappear in innumerability

Zero, without innumerability, is too small
Only innumerability can walk
The vast space of zero
Zero is the mother
The child – innumerability (in the infinity of nothingness)

ZERO

What is zero, a number or nothing, or infinity itself
Is innumerability big enough to fill infinity
Is there a number of innumerability or a number of infinity
Or is infinity a numberless number in its infinity
Where infinity hides and an end in it
Is innumerability in infinity or infinity in innumerability
Does the end hide infinity, or does infinity hide the end
Or does zero count infinity in innumerability
Is zero the end of infinity or infinity the end of zero
Or is zero the infinity of the end in infinity
Does innumerability spread to zero
Or does innumerability have no end
For it always establishes the correspondence between numbers
Is there the final number?
There is neither the final number nor the number of innumerability
In this battle, the number loses, but the new number does not
A number cannot vanquish a number or infinity
Zero plays with both the number and infinity
Zero does not need a number, infinity, or end
But the number, end, and infinity all need zero
Only zero can mark both the end and infinity
Only it can give birth to the final number
Only it knows the true value of the number
Zero is the first and final number
Zero is the alpha and omega of numbers, yet itself not a number –
Smaller than the number, greater than infinity.

THE GERM

Darkness is thicker than darkness
Light brighter than light
A world guarding itself
From the darkness, hides in its darkness
All memory, beauty, movement
Condensed along the very brink of zero.
It dreams of itself in its night
And waits in its sleep.
That small truth bigger than the truth
That something devoid of space and time
Outside space and time
Greater than space and time
It is waiting to annul itself
To be able to see with the eyes of Zero
And then to be born again.
A passage through zero is the creation of the world
A passage through zero is a touch of two essences
A passage through zero is a loving embrace
Of darkness and hidden light
Which is born from that embrace.
When it touches zero
Nothing starts to scream
And to spread within the germ

The germ is not a burst but an expansion – the awakening of atoms by the birth of space. And space is nothing but nothing expanding within the germ, creating distances between atoms that are born. Nothing gives birth to the illusion of space and time – to measure distance, while the germ always remains the same – the truth pumped from within.

THE FATHER

Lonely in the void
And emptiness lonely within him
He owes his absence to the emptiness
And he owes his life to it
Although he is the father, the emptiness is his mother
He gives birth to emptiness, giving her meaning
She gives birth to him, offering him her womb
Offering him a way to jump into himself
Without her, he would not penetrate
Without her, he would be emptiness
Without her, there is no path.
He looks for a path to himself through her;
She embraces him from outside and inside,
All his virility lies in her passivity
Her sterility is his fertility
Her nothingness is her purity.
Only nothing is wholly pure and sinless
And only out of complete purity can he be born
Only emptiness can be so large to receive him
Only emptiness is ready for his violent penetration
Only emptiness can stand his breath
His biggest secret lies in violating the emptiness
And he sends her a kiss
In the form of a scream and bang
And that scream is only seemingly his
It is her bang within him
It is she, waking and expanding inside him
It is she, dissolving him from within
She is a bang
That awakes her son with a scream
She is a violation of his balance and peace

But in his greatest glory
He is a dormant, fixed-point
That's why the mother protests within him
And that's why she sinks into him
The deeper and bigger she is within him
The wider and larger He is
At her other end
On which she faithfully awaits and receives him

THE MOTHER

The lonely emptiness awaits his awakening
She watches him while he sleeps, watches over him when he is
    awake
She gives him life and feeds him
Emptiness is his food
How to describe emptiness, how to describe nothing
How to conjure up the power of a powerless Mother
A Mother whose only strength is the absence of strength
Whose only strength is the ability to receive strength
To expand in strength and her impotence
To allow his omnipotence
Her power is in impotence
Only she is boundless
Only she is everywhere and always
Only she is always in the same place
Only she gives birth
Only she doesn't complain
She is darkness and emptiness

Although everybody fears darkness and emptiness, they pose no danger to anybody. Only light brings beauty and danger – light is an ambiguous force that warms up and destroys. Her son possesses the power, and only power causes fear. Darkness is infinitely peaceful and harmless. Nobody is in danger of darkness and emptiness. Only shape gives birth to danger; only in movement lies life: movement gives birth to shapes and distances. The fear of emptiness is the fear of distance.

THE FATHER AND THE MOTHER

Dispersion of a father is not a real explosion because nothing separates from each other and wanders blindly. An explosion is a burst – a hopeless division of pieces, and this is the body's growth, the organism's development by receiving emptiness and expanding from within. The emptiness dissolves the father – she creates space and time within him; the emptiness outside him is nothing – outside space and time. Without him, emptiness cannot be measured: it is the same everywhere and always in the same place; it has neither length nor height nor width nor duration. Without the father, everything is always in the same place and at the same time.

Only when he wakes up inside her, and she inside him, do distances become possible. That is how the emptiness achieves an illusion of size because it moves among shapes or forms that inhabit her. Only his energy gives birth to the illusion of space, and the illusion of space to the illusion of movement and duration because everything remains in the same place after the emptiness has evaporated from him. His evaporation is not his evaporation but the evaporation of the emptiness from inside him: without her, he is reduced to his basic element; everything returns to the same place and is reduced to the original element. Even if he is dissolved into a multitude of universes, everything arrives at the same place through the evaporation of emptiness; even if from countless different sides, he rushes into countless different directions at infinite distances from each other, he still rushes into nothing.

All directions lead to one point, and all distances join in one place because once he is reduced to himself, there is nothing else than him descended into himself. Without emptiness – wherever he is, he is everywhere; wherever he is, he's in the same place. There is nothing but him in his original element and no other form but for the empty emptiness and him in her, and her in him who at the brinks of zero waits to wake him up again, but without him being dissolved.

When each form returns to its essence, the greatest distance is as close as the closest proximity. If people solve this secret, they will conquer space and time.

In the end – alone and taken away
Turned into nothing – asleep
He waits for nothing to lift him from nothing
So he would spread again
The laws by which birth occurs

DECOMPOSITION

The division is not a real division but a birth
The decomposition of the essence and the Divine solemnity
Emptiness enables growth from nothing
There is nothing more sublime or more powerful
There is nothing more beautiful or more vigorous
Than the smile of the black star that shines
(In the black sea of nothingness)
There are innumerable hopes of dormant light
Dreaming of infinity in her sleep
Only in relations does light make sense
Only in relations do smiles give birth to love
Only in relations is motion possible
Only in relations is there a goal.
The strongest condensed light is the smallest
And the largest condensed magnitude
Is the smallest precisely because it is the largest
Nobody sees its light
Nobody is happy about her magnitude
Nothing revolves around it, and she doesn't revolve around
    anything
Except for the emptiness within God and Him inside her
God does not see his greatness and glory
The omnipotent sense of God has seen everything
Achieved every goal, traveled every path
His only strength lies in the creation
His full size is his death
But God can neither die nor be born
He seeks salvation from His greatness within Himself
He is unhappy with complete equality
He can't escape Himself, for He is one and alone
Aware that the only salvation comes from nothing

Aware that he can't do anything on His own
Aware that Nothing has equal power
He knows that He is the Only Something
He knows that there is nothing beyond Him but nothing
Nothing is something that God rejoices in while dreaming
Nothing is His hope, for he can do nothing by Himself
Only God knows the power of nothingness
He has nothing but Himself and nothing
He has nothing else to rely on
His only leverage is nothing
He seeks nothingness
He gives birth to Himself from a loving embrace with nothing
God is one, but without nothing, he is nothing
Something and nothing is the magical duality of God
Who knows that nothing is equally important

MERGING

A bang is a conquest of space
A decomposition of God
Followed by the merging
The revival of the decomposed being
The energy of the liquid mist becomes a shape
The idea begins its story
Matter is the language of the idea
Atoms are God's alphabet
The world is God's Bible
He talks to everyone
On each conversation and agreement
Each shape depends
The life of an idea is the development of the alphabet
The elements are the alphabet
Compounds – the spelling
A letter shines from every shape
An idea shines from every shape
Every explosion is another note
Giving birth to new elements
On the musical ladder of being
The development of the elements is the memory of being
The path is not traveled
Only the message is transmitted
Space and time are the memory
Of the Decomposed (Being)
Counting innumerability
In self-realization
And the goal of self-realization is the path
Traveling is the sole hope
And there is no travel
Without decomposition and merging

In merging on the path
Lies the charm of summer
The final merging is the end of the road
Achieving the goal is death
He spreads His music
He listens and watches Himself
He is awaiting Himself on the path
He speaks in whispers to Himself
He deceives Himself with beauty

DIVISION AND MERGING

One decomposes itself, and the multitude is layered
There is no real division
But without division, there is no life
The newly decomposed merges and melts
The way of the world is the way of decomposition and merging
Speed enables both
Without speed, there is no decomposition
But without speed, there is neither merging
With speed, one conquers space
Speed groups larger shapes
Mass is a consequence of speed
The gravitational force of larger forms is the sum of the velocity of
    the larger number
Movement (vibration), not mass, creates the force of gravity
Speed maintains balance
Decomposition gives direction and path
Merging sustains life
The world is wholly decomposed at the beginning
To be able to look for itself along the path
One particle speaks in whispers to another
Innumerable particles or innumerable memories
Rush into relations and create relations
From this amorous game, the first forms are born
The world establishes order
Every essence obtains a sense
Everything is maintained in relations
Smaller and larger families are winning their positions
Offering life to emptiness
The life of emptiness is space
Without relations and hierarchy
Nothing could survive

Hierarchy maintains order
The speed of the larger enables the speed of the smaller
Everything rushes toward nothing
But slowly
Without the hierarchy of the universe,
Nothing would ever come to life or last
It is not a question of goodness but survival
Equality means death and ruin
There is no balance in equality
There is nothing to keep families together
To guard, feed, and protect a huge family of infinity and
    innumerability
Eventually, everything decomposes or melts
And returns to the same point (which is the same everywhere)

MOTION

Is there motion
Is the path toward oneself motion
Is there a true division
The path depends on the division
Without a multitude, there are no relations
Without relations, there is no distance
Without distance, there is no creation
Is it movement or flicker
Or is flickering a path remembering
A distance that catches up with itself
In self-realization.
But without division and multitude,
Everything loses its meaning
There is no law without a motion
Gravity does not begin with mass
But with motion
Motion causes speed and rotation
Motion gives birth to energy
Without motion, every energy and every mass
Lose their value
Larger worlds are a consequence of the movement of smaller ones
All the masses were initially the same
Larger masses could not have formed
By attracting masses, but through the speed of the masses
The whole force of the world lies in motion
Larger worlds do not use mass to attract smaller ones
But through the sum of smaller energies in motion
Every step is a path of the idea
Every thought is a dreaming matter
Every particle is a singing idea
Every memory is a revived beauty

Motion is the main source of energy
No dimension exists without motion
Without motion, there is no weight
Mass loses its value with the loss of motion
Everything becomes weightless and light
The basic energy of the universe
Its reason and sense lie in motion
Its chief law, purpose, and rank
Only motion gives birth to hope
Only motion offers consolation
Only motion offers a memory
But also oblivion

IMMOBILITY

The largest world is the most miniature world
It can fit entirely within itself
It contracts by descending into itself
There is virtually no end to its contraction.
There is nothing smaller than the greatest
Sinking into itself.
Infinity of the largest world
Reaches the very point on the brink of zero.
That's where his whole magnitude sleeps.
Everything that is outside of it is enormous in its nothingness
Only nothing can be so enormous
Only nothing has no limits
Only nothing encompasses infinity
But in the same way, nothing has nowhere to go
It has nowhere to go either
It, without anything, hidden within itself
Hidden in nothingness
And nothingness hidden in him
It sleeps motionless
Only sleep warms it
But sleep also requires something else
It has dreamed his every dream to the fullest
It doesn't need itself
It is dumb, blind, and powerless
There is only nothing to keep him company
There is only nothing to awaken its dream
It observes nothing while dreaming
It begs nothing to awaken it
From its darkness
And to lift it high
Nothing gives it speech, sleep, or sight

It's difficult to be alone and enormous
It sinks under its own weight
It dies of its own strength
Its greatest strength ends
In immobility. A slave to its power
And the master of sad nothingness
That it's driven out of itself,
Its victory is its downfall
It defeats itself by defeating nothingness
Alone with itself, within itself, and for itself
It identifies with the defeated side
Both are frozen
Worthless in their helplessness and omnipotence
Both immobile
Any victory between them is temporary
And so is every defeat
There is no struggle between them
There is only their loving embrace
Their every quarrel marks life
Every quarrel between them is a joy
Their quarrel gives birth to light
Power hates its power the most
The mortal enemy of power is its own power
The pinnacle of power is immobility
Its apex is its nadir
It accepts the fall to rejoice in the heights
It accepts the bottom so it can fly
The fall gives birth to its wings
It accepts the darkness that awakens its light
Without darkness, it is darkness
Without the bottom, it's at the bottom
Without nothingness, it is nothingness

RELATIVITY

Everything is in relations; everything touches everything else and seeks and finds itself in relations. The world is an enormous circle of God-Absolute and His stairway on the path from nothing to sense. Every step of his is a part of the universal thread and bloodstream; every atom and star are the nerves of his being. One without the other, they are nothing – just a divided body; it's a symphony of a single being that climbs to the top and bottom of itself. The staircase is his melody; relations are his story – and letters are born, fly, and spread.

The conversation is his essence – everything is in conversation and relation, in an unwritten agreement; everything seeks itself in another with a movement born out of speed. Speed is the power of gravity; with speed, everything is maintained; in speed, there lies the power of balance as everything in motion hurls into nothing towards the very end and beginning:

> The song and conversation last
> As one body swallows another
> As that other body gives birth to yet another
> As one star lights up
> And dies prematurely in the ecstasy of its fire
> To be able to give birth to another star
> So that this other star could live
> So that a new planet would be born
> From the star's new elements
> That bestow life upon others through its death.

There is no real story about space and time except that the world is to evaporate eventually, and it's sad to imagine a disappearing world, even after a hundred to the power of eight trillion years. Was it but a universe expanding inside another? What are the farthest bodies, and can the bodies inaccessible to telescopes be anticipated, and could it be perhaps that what you expect, sensing (seeing) their contours, are universes beyond this one and that all of the universes exist together in another whole of another universe as in this whole of the galaxy? And so on, indefinitely and innumerably. And were there many explosions before the one considered to be initial, and are there other explosions beyond this one from the same void, and is the universe bursting all around, and is everything expanding or contracting into nothing, and is it perhaps that some are expanding, while others are sinking back into themselves and does each of them find their death in the infinite space of zero and does everything reappear in the same place independently of movements and distances? Does that place, or do all places, at some point, become the same place?

Everything returns to the same place
When everything evaporates, time disappears
When everything evaporates, space disappears as well
When space disappears, there is no distance
When there is no distance, everything is in the same place
When everything is in the same place and contracted
Nothing is going anywhere
There is nothing but emptiness –
The same emptiness everywhere
Wherever it goes, it remains in the same place
And so, without space and time,
Wherever it is, it is everywhere
And if it expands or recedes into the distance,
It arrives at the same place
It's in every place
It watches from every place
There is nothing else but it.
And if there used to be many of them
And if every one of them ended up

In expansion or contraction,
Or some in expansion, others in contraction,
They all would eventually reappear in the same place anyway
They are all in every place
They are all at the same time as well
And even if there was only one
Or a large number of them
Everything reaches the same goal
And is always in the same place
At the same time
Only a germ can give birth to space
Without energy, there is no distance
Only while one energy is in pursuit of another
Space and motion are possible
A space devoid of energy is nothing –
A desolate, sizeless void
Only one force can provide another with a reason
While supporting it in movement and wearing out;
All energies are divided by nothing
That is why zero is the most important number
And if nothing is really nothing
Why waste time mastering it
To what purpose does it require steps
Or nothing is merely nothing
Only when it is alone and separated from the germ
When the germ itself is nothing without it
Each of them is both everything and nothing
Always in the same place and at the same time
Beyond space and duration.
When everything dies – nothing dies, too.
Without nothing, life would be nothing;
And death itself would be eternal
And nothing devoid of nothing.
And God cannot die.

He is everything and nothing,
And Nothing can never die.

Notes on the Poems' Creation Dates

Poems written in 2000:

The cycle "The God and the Devil": "The God's Path", "God Is Perfect."

"The Pyramid of the World" (Proemium), 2007.

The rest of the book was written in 2008.

ABOUT THE AUTHOR

Dejan Stojanović was born in Peć in 1959. He graduated from the Law School of the University of Priština. He has published these books of poems:

Circling (Krugovanje), Narodna knjiga – Alfa, Belgrade, three editions – 1993, 1998, and 2000.

The Sun Observes Itself (Sunce sebe gleda), NIP Književna reč, Belgrade, 1999.

The Sign and Its Children (Znak i njegova deca), Prosveta, Belgrade, 2000.

The Creator (Tvoritelj), Narodna knjiga, Belgrade, 2000.

The Shape (Oblik), Gramatik, Podgorica, 2000.

The Dance of Time (Ples vremena), Konras, Belgrade, 2007.

Pentalogy: *The World in Nowherness (Svet u nigdini):*

1. Ozar (Ozar), Udruženje književnika Srbije, Belgrade, 2017.

2. The World and God (Svet i Bog), Udruženje književnika Srbije, Belgrade, 2017.

3. The World in Nowhereness (Svet u nigdini), Udruženje književnika Srbije, 2017.

4. The World and Humans (Svet i ljudi), Udruženje književnika Srbije, Belgrade, 2017.

5. The Home of Light (Dom svetlosti). Udruženje književnika Srbije, Belgrade, 2017.

The Hidden Light (Skrivena svetlost), Čigoja, Belgrade, 2018.

Primordial Spark (Iskra iskona), Albatros plus, Belgrade, 2021.

Centuries and Steps (Vekovi i koraci), Albatros plus, Belgrade, 2023.

Essays:

Creator and Creating (Stvaralac i stvaranje), Albatros plus, Belgrade, 2021.

The New Man and the New World (Novočovek i novosvet), Rad, Belgrade, 2022.

Anthology: *Selected Serbian Plays (Izabrane srpske drame)*, USA, 2016.

Philosophy: *Absolute*, New Avenue Books, USA, 2024.

A book of his selected interviews, Conversations, was published in 1999 by NIP Književna reč, Belgrade. The Serbian Heritage Foundation and the Association of Writers of Serbia for Intellectual Engagement awarded the book the Rastko Petrović Prize.

www.ingramcontent.com/pod-product-compliance
Lightning Source LLC
Chambersburg PA
CBHW020649250626
47154CB00008B/2871